ROSEMARY AND GABRIEL

LAPTOP LOVE

Rosemary and Gabriel

Laptop Love

Janice Moore Fuller
& Janet Lewis

Illustrated by Lauren Faulkenberry

On the Bevel Press

ISBN: 978-1-947834-53-8 (ebook) / 978-1-947834-54-5 (pbk)

Published by On the Bevel Press
Salisbury, NC
Book design and illustrations by Lauren Faulkenberry

ALSO BY JANICE MOORE FULLER

Archeology Is a Destructive Science

Sex Education

Séance

On the Bevel

PRAISE FOR ROSEMARY AND GABRIEL

"Friendship and love in all its forms are the stuff of life that makes us whole. This "tail" of love is tender and hilarious, heartbreaking at times, but ultimately uplifting. It will catch you off guard in all the most wonderful ways. I quite literally laughed out loud at the sly and intelligent humor and then fast on the heels of that emotion, found my hand over my heart and tears pouring from my eyes as I came away from this story of true love with a renewed spirit of my own. Deep, rich and purrfect."

–AMY WILLOUGHBY-BURLE, AUTHOR OF *THE YEAR OF THORNS AND HONEY*

"In this touching and poignant collection of emails written by two cats, Janice Fuller connects the reader to the unique bond created between animals possessing very human and humane sensitivities. Embedded in this humorous correspondence is an intense depth of emotion, exploring friendship in all its stages: delight in discovery and flirtation, the strengthening of the union, and the acceptance of grief and loss. Truly a warm and loving tribute."

–DEBRA A. DANIEL, AUTHOR OF *THE ROSTER*

This sweet book offers an imaginative, charmingly illustrated, delightfully litter-ate cat's-eye view of love, unconsummated longing, birth, rebirth, and, of course, all things feline. Gabriel plays the role of courtly lover in a May/December romance with Rosemary, whose wild abandon with spelling and grammar adds to the fun. Soothing, playful, and poetic. You'll never look at sunbeams the same way again.

–BILL SPENCER, AUTHOR OF *URANUS IS ALWAYS FUNNY*

This inventive epistolary love story between two spunky cats abounds with entrancing surprises—like all magic acts. The lovers, who correspond by pouncing on laptop keys, are rebelling against their parental units, English professors revering James Joyce. In fact, they animate elements of his masterful short novel, *The Dead*. In this winter-to-spring romance, Rosemary, eighteen, and Gabriel, five, bursting with life, become smitten through e-mail. Their intimacy grows as the shadows gather.

Ardent Gabriel, "whiskers bristling with love," embodies the strengths of Joyce's opposites, possessing the brain of Gabriel Conroy and the valor of the ill-fated Michael Furey. Gabriel's acrobatics, as he leaps across the rafters of his home, are matched by Rosemary's frisking with language, including punning and eccentric punctuation. He's attracted by her originality; she's seized by his nobility. Their personalities and antics are admirably captured by the marvelously responsive illustrations of Lauren Faulkenberry.

You will be suffused by the poignancy of this feline romance in the same way that Gretta Conroy remembers being swollen with love for the gallant Michael Furey. But departing from the gloom of Joyce's story, Janice Fuller's wry, zestful, affecting tale offers glimmers of a reunion. If you believe like Gabriel that "humans live to serve cats," you'll be inspired, heart and soul, by this beautiful book—a must for feline fanatics, literati, and lovers of love stories.

–MICHAEL GASPENY, AUTHOR OF *REWRITE MEN* AND *THE TYRANNY OF QUESTIONS*

CONTENTS

Dedicated to the memory

of Janet Lewis (1940-2018)

INTRODUCTION

The idea of a feline love story revealed through emails seemed too far-fetched to me until two cats—my cat Gabriel and Janet Lewis's Rosemary—found each other through technology. Janet was the mother of Catawba College's president, Brien. Through many dinners with Janet and her husband Joe, I discovered that she and I shared important interests. For one, we were both college English professors—with me at Catawba College and Janet at York University in Toronto. As professors, we shared a special affection for James Joyce and Virginia Woolf. We also both loved cats. Janet was intrigued that Gabriel, a buff and white rescue cat, was named after Gabriel Conroy in Joyce's "The Dead." When Janet casually mentioned that Rosemary, also a rescue cat, insisted on capitalizing all Rs (because her name began with a capital R), I knew that Gabriel and I needed to meet her. When Janet handwrote a letter addressed to both Gabriel and me, he became determined to correspond with Rosemary. With his Joycean name, he felt it was his literary duty to pursue a relationship with a cat with an unusual interest in language and a novel way of writing.

Gabriel used to resent my laptop. It consumed so much of my attention on the weekends and evenings. He showed how jealous he was by jumping into my lap and then springing onto my keyboard. In the middle of the night, he would land on the dormant keys sending out *bing, bing, bing* in hopes of waking me up to play. When he was a young cat, he managed to break off the letter Z. Until the keyboard was repaired after considerable time and frustration, I was surprised to discover how often I relied on Z. Honestly, part of Rosemary's interest in email came from our territorial struggle over the laptop, the site of conflict. When Gabriel took a serious interest in communicating with Rosemary, he found that with practice he could control his paws enough to type specific keys. As their email exchange began, the two agreed to honor Rosemary's convention of capitalizing all Rs. But eventually Rosemary, then eighteen years old, admitted that capitalizing all Rs took more energy than she could muster. Though only five years old, Gabriel was relieved to hear this confession. He was finding it taxing and tedious to hold down the caps-shift key at the same time he pressed the key of the desired letter. Of course, he blamed the strain on his lack of balance rather than a deficiency of strength. He suggested that they only capitalize Rs in their names and in the salutations and closings.

Despite this concession, Rosemary was rebellious. She didn't mind violating the rules that English presented. In fact, she was defiant. She boldly misspelled. She found typos humorous and proofreading monotonous. Gabriel, like his name-sake Gabriel Conroy, was aware of the power of language and defended Rosemary's "errors" as linguistic insurrection, worthy of William Blake and Emily Dickinson.

Janet and I were originally vexed that our cats fiddled with the computers. It wasn't unusual for Janet to shoo Rosemary from the keyboard. I sometimes rushed Gabriel from the laptop by clanging together pots and pans. Eventually, though, we came to appreciate the email exchange for the lovely courtship it was. We began to leave our computers turned on and our email accounts open for the epistolary story that follows.

I. FIRST MEETING

I make lots of errors, but
errors can be exciting.

With best wishes,
RosemaRy

To: RosemaRy <ProfJaLewis@yahoo.com>
From: Gabriel <JniceFul25@gmail.com>
Date: January 8
Subject: Introduction

Greetings, RosemaRy.

Kindly thank your mother for her paw-written letter. It was addressed in part to me. My mother (otherwise known as "the Human") brought it to me today, nearly a month after your mother posted it. Apparently, my mother didn't check her college mailbox during the holidays and just discovered your letter today. (Humans!)

When your mother Janet told my mother Janice that you capitalize all Rs because your name begins with a capital R, I knew I needed to meet you. This "loft" where we live is spacious, but it can be a lonely, if lofty place. I hope we can become exceptional friends. If our college-professor mothers can connect on literary matters, we can certainly forge a relationship.

Today my human leader/mother left her computer and email on while she went to the grocery store. Even when the computer is turned off, I have been practicing using my nimble paws so that I can effectively email you. So now that the opportunity has arrived, I am here pushing down the keys and hoping I can send you my thoughts.

With Respect and cuRiosity,

GabRiel

P.S. I have decided to honor your convention of capitalizing all Rs. I must confess that pressing the shift key so often can be somewhat onerous.

~

To: Gabriel <JniceFul25@gmail.com>
From: RosemaRy <ProfJaLewis@yahoo.com>
Date: January 8
Subject: A Canadian Hello

Greetings, GabRiel!

How nice to get an email from you. My leaders don't mind that I stand on their computer keys and tyyyype. Repeated letters are sometimes cheeery and easy to do. They don't seem to mind that I'm acatually compooosing an email to their friend Janice's caaaat—click, click, cliiiiccck!

I am happy to start writing back and forth. I'll try to make sure that you can read what I write. I make lots of errors, but errors can be exciting. As for my love of the letter R, let's ugree to only use capitals in the greeting and closing. For an 18 yr. old cat, I'm pretty nimble, as you call it, but reaching the shifttt key while hitting alphabet keys uses feline enrgy (paw! pow! paw!) that I need to save for something else.

I'm sorry you don't have animal companionship. Nikita and me sees lots animalss, incluging the dawg next door; he is acsually quite nice and wants to be friends but I dont wants to lower my social status.

We have lots of raccoons in Toronnto. do you have them in Carolina, North? I chase them away.

With best wisshes foR ouR canadiun-ameRicaan fRiendship,

RosemaRy

~

To: RosemaRy <ProfJaLewis@yahoo.com>
From: Gabriel <JniceFul25@gmail.com>
Date: January 9
Subject: The Beauty of Fur

DeaRest pRospective fRiend RosemaRy,

Today my mother turned on something that looked like a tiny tv with flashing pictures. After many boring pictures of humans (and some skeletons!), I finally got to see your pictures and pictures of your sister Nikita. I must say I am smitten with you! You are so beautiful with your Gabriel-colored fur, and you have the sweetest face and eyes. Could I possibly court you?

I wish my fur were as long as yours! My mother keeps the thermostat pretty low! I would value some long, warm fur! The lion-mane look is so appealing!

My mother has just arrived home and is making me get off the keyboard and back onto the floor. Does she not see that I'm emailing you? I think she does, but she says she must finish her lesson plans for tomorrow's classes. Boring!

I just reread your letter. I see that you mention a brother. Is Nikita a boy? My mother misled me on this, I think. Apparently, she once saw a film about a woman named Nikita. More later. I'm curling up on the bed right now.

PuRR and puRRRR again!

GabRiel

~

To: Gabriel <JniceFul25@gmail.com>
From: RosemaRy <ProfJaLewis@yahoo.com>
Date: January 9
Subject: Humane Society White Sale

Hello, Gabe, my handsome feline coRRespondent!

Yes, Nikita was origunally a boy. His cojones was missing when he moved in. So was his rear leg. The Tail missing is part of his Manx ancestors. His name was Nyka at his former home and in his dim way he seemed to recogngize it. My mum thought it sounded like an athletic shoe, and, when she called him Nikita after the former Russian premier, he answered to that too. Lots of peoples think its a girls name. He is my (gag) brother. So is the human Brien, aka Bear. As a result, I am the aunt of a cockapoo (the expensively spoiled Lucy). Interspecial reelations are strange, arenut they? Nik is friends with the racoons. When his pal Skunky got runned over by a car, he rolled on his body and got very stinky.

Shortly after we moved to this house in Toronto, a couple of Russian sailors who had jumped ship came by to shovvel snow. One of them spoke good English and it was a heavy shovvelling job so they had supper with us. Lovely guys. The youngest had orang hair and was named Nikita and so he loved our Nik and spoke Russian to him. Instant bonding.

My beautiful fur is pewter and white. The day we comed home frum the Humane Sussiety, they were havings a white sale (anyone who had white fur was 50% off) and mum claimed Nik's whiskers counted so he was on sale too. Actsually they were tryings to gets rid of everybuddy....... imagine!

I'll be thinking about your offer to court me; I am very fussy and you are so much younger.

Chastely, RosemaRy

~

To: RosemaRy <ProfJaLewis@yahoo.com>
From: Gabriel <JniceFul25@gmail.com>
Date: January 15
Subject: This and That

Hi, RosemaRy. I like the sound of pewter. It's beautiful. The shelter ad said my coat is buff. I prefer to think of it as cinnamon or dusty peach.

I love your name, RosemaRy, but would you mind if I sometimes call you Rosie?

My mother let me look at a James Joyce book about a cat and the devil. Your mother sent it to her. In it, the devil tricks the mayor's cat into falling in the river. I hate getting wet. That poor cat.

But in the end I like devils better than mayors, don't you? Sometimes I think my mother is a devil, and I don't mind. Tell Nikita hello for me. I think a "white sale" for pets is an intriguing idea.

My mother is charging toward the keyboard right now, banging a pot lid against a pot, to make me get down. She says she has to go to school.

Those poor crows outside my window. They need to expand their linguistic range, don't you think? It's not that hard to roll an r. I have no trouble saying trrrrrrrruck.

Purrr, pewterrrrr, purrrfect.

GabRRRRRiel

~

To: Gabriel <JniceFul25@gmail.com>
From: RosemaRy <ProfJaLewis@yahoo.com>
Date: January 15
Subject: Beauty and Books

DeaR GabRiel,

Yes, you may call me Rosie. I is temporarily not beutiful. All my lovely fur is shaved off ecxept for my head. Over xmas I got fur matts like a buffalo. Mom's hands dont work sissors so good and Daddy cut my skin; he was very very sorry; so was I. The vet clipped me all over and said I should stay inside. I loook like Twiggy after a bad hair cut. I wasunt eating much and couldunt groom myself. So now I have 2 kinds of medicine and a pilll every day.

Daddy thot it was the Final Exit for me but my kidnies is not tooo bad. Mum hid the bill or Id be getting funeral bills.

Did you nkow I speaks Spanish, and French sometimes. Last night Down-town Abby was on the TandV in French but daddy turned to the fecking curling. A horrible game on ice with brooms. Boring. They yell all the time.

The cat and the devil book is kinda simple minded and too wet. Our neighbor Cathy's book is much funnier but with sad places. She autogrfed my copy becase I sit under her bird feeeder. So does Nik but hes not a book collector like me. I have a silly boook about yoga for cats. Funny pictures. You need 4 legs to do yoga so its no good for Nik.

Does yore mother write pomes about cats?

Have you been fixt? I dont mind, Im just taking precautions.

SinceRly,

R

II. LOVE IN THE TIME OF ILLNESS

Do something
each day that
terrifies you.

To: RosemaRy <ProfJaLewis@yahoo.com>
From: Gabriel <JniceFul25@gmail.com>
Date: January 19
Subject: Questions about Romance

Dear RosemaRy,

I have been fixed. I don't want you to worry on that account.

I have two human sisters Alison and Megan. I am not privy to their romantic/sexual business, but I do know that Megan has not been fixed. She has a kitten in her belly. It's funny that humans don't generally have litters of kittens. Megan's one kitten (a girl) has to be inside Megan for an inordinate amount of time—nine months. Strange, isn't it?

Knowing the human patterns of off-line courtship, I don't think you'll mind if I ask questions about romance—brushing paws, swishing tails, and pressing a nose to the screen. I hope you aren't offended by my curiosity.

Romantically youRs,

GabRiel

~

To: Gabriel <JniceFul25@gmail.com>
From: RosemaRy <ProfJaLewis@yahoo.com>
Date: January 19
Subject: When It's Time To Quit

Hi, GabRiel.

I usually dont kiss on a first date or after only a few emails but I'mm going to relax my standards. To be blunt, old hoss, I'm on my way out, as in cat hell or heaven or the great catnip valhalla in the sky. The Vet this am was pleased I have gained 2 lbs but not happy I have water in my rrear legs and a tumour inside. He says I have a few weeks left.

Daddy would probably pull the plug but says it's Mummy's decesion (safe male out—she gets stuck with the probable-shit decisions) so we had a chat and she said all the previous animals told her when it was time to quit and as I am still perky and purring, we could hang on until I'm ready. No consumtive fade-out; I shall leave with my beautiful tail up.

So you will have to swing on the rafters without much future correspondunce, unless there is Celestial Google or seances like your mummmmy writes about. Nikita may pick up the writing but he is stupid. Reallly STOOPID. His reaction —"duh, will I be the only cat? Will I get all the food?" I'd be pissed off to leave him in charge. His interests will never match up with mine.

Yeah it has been cold outside but now it's raining and the snow is melting and freezing and there are puddles. I dont go out because my beautiful fur is shaved off and it is no trouble to use the litter box. My human bruther Bear (a.k.a. Brien) called us. Lucy the blondenitwit dog is chassing squrrels and Kudzu is playing basketsballs. I dont goes ner the fone when the humans talk because someone mite pull my beautiful tail to make me meow in the fone. How gross.

I dont has much other news. I am glad you electd Presidunt O'Bama even if he has a dawg. I likes tall, dark, and hansum Irishmen. (And I'm named after an Irishman.) You must be Irish evun if you arnt tall and dark.

Party on,

Rosie

To: RosemaRy <ProfJaLewis@yahoo.com>
From: Gabriel <JniceFul25@gmail.com>
Date: January 31
Subject: Joyce, Snow, and Nora

Oh, my dearest Rosie,

I am immeasurably sad to get your email. (I know that sounds pretentious, but I mean it. Plus I like to use the words I look up in my mother's Oxford English Dictionary.) I cannot believe that what you tell me is true. We have just become sweethearts. We haven't had time to scratch furniture together or race across the rafters here in my mother's loft. I know you probably couldn't come here, but I was beginning to dream of it. I wish I could see you while you're still perky and purring, my sweet one.

My mother has confessed that she has been reading our correspondence. Last week she told me she thought you are earthy. I didn't understand what she meant. I haven't touched the earth in years and years, locked as I am (no, hermetically sealed as I am) in this brick and glass box. She rambled for a while about a woman with a nautical name... Nora...Barnacle. She reminded me that I was named after a vacuum-packed, OED-reading man in a story by that fellow Joyce who wrote the cat and devil book. She seems to think you and I were destined for each other.

Yesterday after she read your email, she seemed sad all day, even though she was racing from one thing to another. Late last night when she was getting ready to teach that big bearded man's poetry—Walt somebody—she read me these words: "I bequeath myself to the dirt to grow from the grass I love, If you want me again look for me under your boot soles." Is that what they will do? Bequeath (OED) you to the dirt? I can't get outside to touch the grass. But maybe my mother will bring a handful inside for me. Or will they release you into the air, where you can blend with the wind and the rain and the snow. Oh, the snow! I saw snow on my windowsill last week, and you will maybe have another snow soon. My mother keeps talking about the snow being "general" in Ireland. Something about a woman thinking about the snow covering the grave of some kind of furious man she always, always loved. She was babbling, and now I'm meowing things that don't quite make sense. I'll look for you in the snow...?

Until then we will romance each other in words borrowed from those humans. I don't know how to kiss by computer, do you? But I'm determined to do it. I've just rubbed my scent against the keyboard—aosdthi[awebjp—and now I'm touching...touching...just barely touching the screen with the tip of my tail. Gently. Just a touch. A touch. And again.

Love,

GabRiel

To: Gabriel <JniceFul25@gmail.com>
From: RosemaRy <ProfJaLewis@yahoo.com>
Date: January 31
Subject: The Bittersweet and the Sunbeam

Gabe, you are very sweet and romantic. My mother let my aunty Ruth read our coreps... letters and she thought an endd of life love affair was very elegant. To be fair, my end of life is much more extended than most. I am at least 18. About 94 in people years altho I dont look it. I was sorta grown up and had a loitter of illagitimite kittuns before I moved in here. No trace of the kittens but I dount really remember.

I am, as your mother seys, earthy. My mother, before she joyced, wrote about the wife of bath so there is a long connexuion...but I dint have no 5 husnands. I hasnt really had boyfriends before so maybe I am better off with you in a courtly-love unattainable-lady sort of way. I do appreciate the nose touch on the computer, very tender. So much more romantic than a yowl together on a fence esp. as you are an inside cat.

Snow aint all that its cracked up to be, esp. in April with its bitter sweet. It can look pretty on trees and xmas cards but its cold and wet on the paws and bum. And wind aint always for skylarks! Expect I'll go up in smoke like a hindoo but not bathed in the gangees (too wet and dirty). Digging into the permafrost sounds kinda chilly.

So I plan to come back as a sunbeam—not a 90 degree, pass the airconditioning heat wave. I cant imagin doing aerobics on your rafters. I am dainty and agile, but there are limits. I can imagine you up there like a feline Evil Knevil doing wheelees. Very impressive.

I am so hungry. They are feeding me prenizone-kinda stuff and an appetizer-stimulator. I can use 5 square meels a day; they dont have to be square. I could handle a large raw liver pizza. Dont bring grass into the house on behalf of me. Thats illegal. Just when a sunbeam comes in and shows you how dirty the window is, wave a paw in my direction. After all we has 9 lives.

Its kind of you and your mummy to feel sad and think whitman thoughts about me but not being one for paradise or purgatory, let alone hell, I shall opt for a stroll on the Prime Mobile, looking down like Troilus on the litle erthe and all the planets, undisturbed by diving asteroids and television commercials. When the train whistles, think of my travel oppportuneities.

You gotta plan ahead for when Megun has kittens and you'll have to train them; you'll have to head for the high beams or they'll pull your tail. You will be busy.

Thank you for your loving thoughts and sentiments; keep your nose clean.

Smootchies, Rosie.

P.S. Fer hevenssake dont scratch the furniture. That will git you into “big, fat twouble” as a small friend advises. When in need of relief, head for your dish and rattle it, as ever, R

To: RosemaRy <ProfJaLewis@yahoo.com>
From: Gabriel <JniceFul25@gmail.com>
Date: February 1
Subject: Feline Evil Kneivel

DeaRest RosemaRy, Rosie, NoRa,

When I read your messages last night, I laughed out loud, but I was also terribly sad. I tried to write, but everything felt heavy. My mother is heading out to her human “work” (whatever that is), and a friend of hers is coming to visit for the weekend. I don’t know when she’ll turn the computer on for me again. You may wonder how I can pull out the volumes of the OED and drag the magnifying glass into place and not be able to turn on the computer. I wonder that too. Maybe an old superstition of some sort. I’ll try to do it myself this weekend.

My mother has a magnet on the refrigerator that quotes Eleanor Roosevelt: "Do something that terrifies you each day." (It turns out that Eleanor may not be the one who said it but that's ok.) Nothing terrifies me very much. (My heart almost exploded when you referred to me as the feline Evil Kneivel. I've been swaggering across the beams ever since.) But today I will try to master the silver monster laptop by myself. If I don't triumph, I'll have to wait until my mother isn't "busy."

Hold your tail erect, my love. I brush your words on the screen with the tip of my soft tail.

A puRRRfect kiss...

Gabe

~

To: Gabriel <JniceFul25@gmail.com>
From: RosemaRy <ProfJaLewis@yahoo.com>
Date: February 1
Subject: How Not To Be Bullied

Aw you sweetguy, a magician with the OED, a master of aerial achievements. You must be busy entertaining the visitor. Its a snap if the person is pleasant and appreciates cats. If not, you`ve got to jump on the lap and pillow, purr and shed on the clothes, try to poop on the dinner plate.

When my mum was a young girl her obnoxus bully of an uncle came and the cat (a schizo named Dainty-Fury who answered to both or eirthur) strolled over and threww up on his shoes. Mummy then trained herself to barf on command —a very useful trick. I once got carsick but just a bit; I never poop or pee at will, unlike my stoopid in-continent brother Nik. He is DISgusting.

Kisses, Rosie.

~

To: RosemaRy <ProfJaLewis@yahoo.com>
From: Gabriel <JniceFul25@gmail.com>
Date: February 9
Subject: Feline Family

My dearest Rosie,

I told you I would be brave and try to turn on the computer myself this weekend. Well, so far it's not going too well. I think I just sent you a blank message. Let's think of it as the snow that covers the living and the dead. I'll try to aosdaiogh189 across the keys and still make sense. When my mother catches me doing this, she'll probably change the password, whatever that means...

My mother has noticed that you don't often use an apostrophe in the word it's. Actually, it makes sense to save the energy that the apostrophe requires. The possessive pronouns yours, ours, hers, and theirs don't use an apostrophe. From context, the reader can tell its (belonging to it) from its it is. We will ignore my mother's insistence on correctness.

My mother tells me that your fur is beginning to grow back. Even though I knew I'd like the punk look, I'll bet you are even more beautiful now. Have I told you yet how much I enjoy your sense of humor? The story about Dainty-Fury made me laugh and laugh. My mother is entirely too serious about everything. It's nice to have someone in the family who is witty.

I say family, and here's why. My mother and I both see the animals we love as part of our family. When someone says, "but it's just a cat," my mother starts clawing the furniture just as much as I do. I've even heard her say, "What do you know about anything? You're just a human!" My point is that I would have liked to have had you as part of my family. My mother is an only child, and, even though I have two human sisters, they live so far away.

And I've never had children myself, but I wish we could find your kittens and see how they turned out. I'm so glad you mentioned my sister Megan's kitten (and maybe there will be more later!) Yes, I'll help train her. I'll show her how to play with a baby aubergine and how to balance on those high beams. I think I'll be a good father figure. Someone said they saw a mouse in the basement. If only the kitten and I could get loose to chase it. I'm getting better at darting out the door when my mother comes home, especially when she's dragging a bag of student papers with her.

I've already started thinking about you and your travels whenever a train shakes the building and whistles its whistle. Each blast causes me to jump to the window to look for a sunbeam or a raindrop that might be you. And, from now on, whenever I think I see you, I will send a blank email in your honor. When I write an actual email and have to hold down the caps key while the other paw does all the typing, I will capitalize only the Rs in our names and in the salutations and closings (e.g. DeaR and YouRs TRuly).

TendeR love,

GabRiel

~

To: Gabriel <JniceFul25@gmail.com>
From: RosemaRy <ProfJaLewis@yahoo.com>
Date: February 11
Subject: An Unclaimed Treasure

Hi Gabe. I'm still here and eating up nice things. Even my Daddy is treating me like an expensive guest. My stoopid brother has been pooping on the front porch because we had deep snow and now it is melting and there are Big Puddles, so there's this mound of poops that someone will have to round up before tomorrow morning when the garbage man comes.

I havent been doing much, not even watching the first half of Downtown abby because my people went out and didunt leave the tv on. I am not a big tv watcher but myn earlier cat-sister Margaret was. She loved the Blue Jays what are our baseballs team. The tv is on the third floor at the back and all the racoons would line up on the deck and watch too thrugh the glasss dor. A long time ago the blue jays was in the whirled series and my parents were at a play; they didunt leave on the Tv and Margaret was goingnuts. She new they had wone becusae all the cars were tooting threr horns but she didnt know which players had been important. Frum then on they left the tv on but i dont know if they ever winned the whirled series agin. Anyway Mr Bates seems to hav got out of gaol and LadyMerry is getting nocked up.

It is nice that you think of my kittuns but it is soo long ago I has forgetted them. I prefurs to think of me as a unclaimed treasure, untill you, of corse.

FoR my gentleman cat and love,

RosemaRy

III. BE MINE

With trembling whiskers and much love,
Gabriel

To: Gabriel <JniceFul25@gmail.com>
From: RosemaRy <ProfJaLewis@yahoo.com>
Date: February 13
Subject: How To Speak of Love

Hello. Me again! (still; encore/toujours!) I has not had a real boyfriend (I should say a significant unrelated gentleman attacthment) before and so I dont know exactly what to say. And I dont want to seem forword or a huzzy in declaring the secrets of my heart or seem pushy. And becaus we havnt met yet. So I looked in a cat love book and tried to find a sample. Nothing very helpfull as they were playing hard-to-get or too eager to consumate. There was a lot of pounding hearts, violent trembling, storm-tossed fur. Not good since you are a inside cat and anyway the cat in the letter got stood up and she signed herself "lonely kitty" so no good at all. So I will just say

> *Dear Valentine: Roses are red and catnip is blue.*
> *My dear sweet, I purrrrrrrrrrrrrr for you.*

Or how about this?

> *Up in the rafters or chasing a toy,*
> *you are surely a wonderful guy.*

Doesnt quite rhyme...Vers libre? Sounds naughty. Please forgive me for insulting you.

I kiss you Round our whiskeRs.

RosemaRy.

P.S. Regards to your poetical Mummy, just so this affair is out-in-the open, i.e. respectyfull. R

To: RosemaRy <ProfJaLewis@yahoo.com>
From: Gabriel <JniceFul25@gmail.com>
Date: February 13
Subject: Literary Love

Oh, my deaR RosemaRy.

I have never, ever gotten a valentine. I don't think my mother has either. She seems to get really grumpy around this time of year. But I won't let her disdain for the holiday keep me from expressing my love for you.

You are a wonderful poet, my lovely friend. (I like your poems better than my mother's tail-chasing, never-say-what you mean ones! But please don't tell her that. I try to humor her and listen from the windowsill as she reads me various drafts. Yawn...Stretch my paws in front of me. Arch my back.) I love your Roses are red lines. (Literary traditions are important!) I think they might call "purrrrrr" onomatoepooeeeeia. (Spell check doesn't work on this computer. It's too early in the day to fool with the heavy OED.)

And how wonderful that you have a cat love book!! I like the wind lines. Don't worry about my trapped, airless condition. Last night I sat under the ceiling fan trying to simulate the trembling whiskers of cat love. My heart trembled a bit, thinking about you so far away. I have tried to pull out some of my mother's literature books to find something powerful enough to say what I need to meow to you on this special day. Everything I found seemed silly... "How do I love thee, let me pounce on the ways..." "My love is like a pewter, pewter fur ball..." So I've cheated and hacked into my mother's emails. Mr. Garrison Keillor sent her some kind of writing almanac thing this week. And guess whose words were there! the devil man Joyce's. I've adapted a bit of one of his letters to Nora Barnacle for you:

"You are my only love. You have me completely in your power...There is not a whisker of my love that is not yours... Anyhow, NoRa-Rosie, I love you. I cannot live without you. I would like to give you everything that is mine—my purple ball with the bell inside, my scratching post, my catnip mouse, the shriveled aubergine I've stuck in the corner, the metallic package of treats my mother hides in the drawer. I would like to go through life side by side with you, fur against fur, until the hour should come for us to die. Even now the tears rush to my eyes and yowls choke my throat as I paw the keys. RosemaRy, we have only one short life in which to love." But we are stretching the days, stretching the days, aren't we?

Roses are red. Old aubergines are blue.
I'll perch on top of the raised piano lid for you.

With trembling whiskers and much love,

Gabe

P.S. I've attached my mother's baby aubergine poem about me. It may give you a glimpse of how charming I can be in person.

My Cat Steals a Baby Aubergine

He will not leave them alone,
crowded in their open carton
from the farmer's market.

I turn to heat the oil. He grabs
a stem with his teeth,
scampers away. He bats it along

between his paws like a soccer ball.
I retrieve it unbruised. We begin again.
One thumps to the hardwood

and he's off and running.
He hides it from himself behind
the sofa leg, strolls away, feigns

forgetfulness, then notices it anew
and pounces. Just now, he lies nonchalant
on the floor. No sign of his purple egg.

Where is it? *I ask.* Your toy?
It's covered by his giant paw,
like the pea in a shell game.

When I look again, it's gone.
Hoping to pilfer another,

he gives me a long blank stare.

To: Gabriel <JniceFul25@gmail.com>
From: RosemaRy <ProfJaLewis@yahoo.com>
Date: February 14
Subject: Street Smart

DeaRest GabRiel,

I think you have just sent me one of the loongest valentine emails ever writtn. I guess it must need to be long to show how clevr and handsom you are. I'm glad to send you your first valentine. Don't be sad about the future. You are charming and smart. And don't talk about strtching the days. That sounds like physical education. Have you noticed that I'm soundding like my motheer Janet? The literature professor who knows too much to be very intereesting. That's not true though—my mother is the smartest mosst intereesting human animal I know!! I, on the other hand, am street-cat smart. Take me or leave me. No, no, don't leave me.

With tRue feline love,

RosemaRy

IV. NAMES AND COUNTING LIVES

Where do I even start?

To: RosemaRy <ProfJaLewis@yahoo.com>
From: Gabriel <JniceFul25@gmail.com>
Date: February 23
Subject: Slowly Counting Lives

My deaRest RosemaRy,

Please forgive me for my silence. (A week is much longer in cat days, isn't it?) Your parents may have told you that my mother and I live in a big brick box divided into ten big cat carriers. Last week my mother found out that the woman who has watched over this building, as they call it, has been very, very ill. Let me say this in a gentle, poetic way: she was in a hospital, they've called in hospice, and she's hoping for hospitality wherever she goes next.

So many lovely "hosp" words. I dragged out the OED again. The tiny, tiny print says a hospice is "a house of rest and entertainment for pilgrims and travelers." (It also mentions strangers.) What a nice place that must be. I'm puzzled as to why my mother seems sad. I don't get to travel much (only to the vet's office), but I love it when people stop here in our loft to rest so I can entertain them by climbing the piano and racing up and down the stairs. Is this loft a hospice? Is your home a hospice? I hope so, my sweet RosemaRy. That would make me glad.

Anyway, my mother has kept me awake at night for a week tossing and turning and saying things in her sleep like, "Things fall apart. The center cannot hold." But I think she may have finally, finally found a good helper to take the woman's place. She has said to me, "After the big meeting of owners on Monday afternoon, I'll be able to go back to normal." That doesn't make any sense to me. She has never been normal. I must say, though, that her worries about Megan's kitten are fairly normal. I think grandmothers-to-be often worry about the hospitality of the hospital where kittens are born.

I am so happy that you have reminded me about our nine lives. I will definitely count them. I'm good at words but not so good with counting. I asked my mother to help me count my lives. She said that when she's normal again she will buy me a big abacus like humans use in China and Africa to count things. If I don't let her cut my claws while I'm taking a nap, I should be able to push the beads across the wire, one by one. But I have a question that might seem silly...How do I know what number life I'm living now? How many beads do I push over to the side before I start counting? I asked my mother and she said I was being too much of a literalist. (As an indoor cat, I understand litter but literalist? I won't pull the damned heavy OED out again so soon. Maybe another day.) She says when she hears you saying we have nine lives, she thinks about the crazy poet from Wales that she will talk about in class this week. Apparently he says, no, he shouts, "And death shall have no dominion!" That's a nice thought too, dear RosemaRy, isn't it? But I think I prefer counting beads.

And when you and I finish counting our allotted beads, I think we'll find more somewhere, don't you? I only hope we are together as we keep counting. One...one...one...one...We can count very slowly, my love.

Gabe

To: Gabriel <JniceFul25@gmail.com>
From: RosemaRy <ProfJaLewis@yahoo.com>
Date: February 23
Subject: Heritage

DeaRest GabRiel:

How lovely to hear from you. What a busy life you lead! Sick friends in a hosp-ice, mathematical training in the future, Megan's kitten growing, preparing DillAnn's pomes. My daddy's name is welsh; he has a red dragon flag what we fly at the coootedge and a signet ring (my mummy says he stol it off a dead client) and pretends to be welsh and sings Men of Hair Lick, (Daddy says) but it was the name given to his old uncle when he comed from russia-ukraine/ belarus over a hundred yrs ago.

My muther says her ancester King Brian Boru (who died at Clontarf in 1014 when he alsmost drove the heathunmen--vikings—out of Ireland) was a HIGH KING who my bruther Bear was named after. All the O'Briuns are kings sons who wernt exactly top drawer but they used ther own names even if they wer hanged for sheep-steeling or died of colera digging the Rideau canal in the otttawa valley. In the otttawa vlay, ther was "lace curtain Irush" and "black Irush" becuase they was lumbermen or coal miners and we nevr had no lace curtains excpt my granfather's muther who was scottish and had certuns but no money because her uselushusband drinked it al. Sorry, my family history is somewhat disapointing but after all, I was adopted from the humane society so Idonknow.

I dont think my hous is a hosp-anything. The food has inprovd since I has been “in a decline“ and i can slepp in all my favrite places like mummys head and daddy’s arms (general location). I dont now about counttting; I just count my 4 paws and my brothers 3 paws and my tail and he has a tail so that is 8 so i figger I am in my oneth life. Hard to tell. Antway I am sure you and I will match up somewheres along the way....

My father’s stepmother had a private language. A civil servent was a sitter; a beard was a drape; a little kid was excess baggage and so forth. She laffed like a hyhena and stuck bows on yer head. A real embareassment. She died several years ago and her ashes wer in the trunk of the funerall guys trunk. Last week, the guy phoned my daddy and sed he was getting low on storage space so my parents went and got her. Many inturesting discussions about where to put the ashes. (NOT WITH MINE!!!!!!!)

It is supper time so I gotta check out my dish....

Lots of love,

RosemaRy

~

To: RosemaRy <ProfJaLewis@yahoo.com>
From: Gabriel <JniceFul25@gmail.com>
Date: March 3
Subject: Heritage, Part Two

My deaR RosemaRy!

It's been another "busy" week for my mother/Leader. (What does she have to do? I don't see her cleaning her fur or chasing balls or climbing rafters. She just seems to lean over various piles of paper. . . What a sad, safe life!) Anyway, she just turned on the computer and left to get something from her automobile. So I pounced!

It made me joyful to hear from you. You are one of the funniest creatures I have ever known. I don't know why my mother needs to read all those heavy books. If she'd just read your accounts of these ancestors, she'd have enough entertainment to keep her going for a long time. You sometimes make me laugh and purr out loud at the same time.

My mother says her "people" were Scots Irish and English. I think she wishes she were also Welsh like your daddy. (Why can't she pretend too?) For the past couple of days she's been rushing around talking to a friend in Wales about a trip she'll take in a year with some students to study that Dylan Thomas human. She's excited but also "busy, busy, busy." (She says that's an expression an American writing man named Kurt Vonnegut used in one of his books to talk about useless, frenzied activity. I'm not sure she sees how frenzied and useless some of her rushing around seems to me. She's as bad as those dogs that chase their tails. Don't they annoy you?!) As she's done her planning this week, I actually heard her talk about Hair Lick Castle! She's been there before, she says! Of course, she won't take me along, but I like to think about the fact that you and I have a hair licking connection!

Your own ancestry is certainly not disappointing! After all, those of us who are adopted can invent and reinvent ourselves whenever we want! Oh, think about how different and exotic each of our nine lives can be! All I know about my relatives is this: We kittens were found in a drain. The people at the shelter named us the Professor, Skipper, Ginger, and Marianne--all names from a stupid American tv show about a middle-class, goofy American man named Gilligan! I was supposed to be Skipper! Thank god my mother decided to change my name to the angelic and Irish name GabRiel!

But here's a secret I'll share with you: My mother finally revealed to me not too long ago that she didn't really like the character Gabriel Conroy in the story "The Dead" (by the devil man James Joyce) nearly as much as she liked Michael Furey. (She almost named me Michael but that was her ex-husband's name!) She said Gabriel was pedantic and preferred to be safe and comfortable inside his house, and he would only go out in the snow if he wore galoshes. Can you imagine the shock this secret was to me? Do you think giving me that name has caused me to care too much about the OED and has caused me to be content only to sit in the window and watch the rain and birds and tornadoes from my cozy world?

I won't stand for it. I'm determined to be a different cat. I will be a rash cat. (I see that I'm already writing short, direct sentences like Hemingway!) I've devised a plan. Soon, dear RosemaRy, I'm going to charge past my mother into the hallway, hide in the garage until someone opens the electric door. And then I'm going to race north, north, north through ice storms and sheets of rain and hurricanes, over highways, under bridges, over frozen tundras, through showers of fiery arrows until I come to the Ottawa Valley and Toronto. And then, like Michael Furey, I'm going to stand in the chilly March rain outside your window and meow and meow and meow until you hear me. And then you'll look outside and find me shivering but brave. You'll know then how much I love you.

With love and excitement foR my journey!

Gabe

P.S. Is Toronto very far from Salisbury? Can you send me a map or an atlas or maybe a paw-sized GPS?

~

To: Gabriel <JniceFul25@gmail.com>
From: RosemaRy <ProfJaLewis@yahoo.com>
Date: March 4
Subject: Job Description

My DeaR Gabe,

Dont knock your name. Gabriel the angel had to break the news to Mary that she was going to have that unusual baby and he did so very calmly. That coldhav been nasty but he was very diplomatic.

How is Megan's kittun coming along. You will want to be on hand for that. Maybe you will be the godfather. Not like marlon Brando—the other kind.

My bruther Bear said he was going to do his moocow act from Joyce's *A Portrait of an Artist as a Young Man* at your Leader's class but maybe that was a big fat fib. Did he recite about wetting the bed and the eye-pokin eagles? Or did he try the villllandelle? Such a showoff. My mummmmy used to tell the easter story about poor baby Jesus getting wrapped up in tissue paper and then waking up in the tomb and walking out.

Not much new around here. My newphew Josh is going to Dublin. Mummy ses not to kiss the belarny stone becaus of hoofandmouth disease and the clapp. I'll bet your Leader could give him advice. My parental units are probably going to Sallysbury in April. Daddy is busy rounding up all his friends. God help us if he ever reprises the Canterbury Tails. Mummy sasy she wont go if I am Sick or else she will take me with her. Who knows? Maybe I will be all better and our frend Rosalyn will catsit or maybe I will ben daid. Who knows? Lusydog would have a hissy fit if she mus not chase me.

My Sweetiepie. Daddy is wtching the tv news and I must go and sit on his lap—part of my jobdiscriptiun. At least I keep up to date...

Tenderest of whisker touches.

Much lov, Rosie

V. PHOTOGRAPHS

Standing out in the elements,
like Michael Furey

To: Gabriel <JniceFul25@gmail.com>
From: RosemaRy <ProfJaLewis@yahoo.com>
Date: March 4
Subject: The Necessity of Goloshes

Dearest Gabe: so much news. My muthers frend, Anty Ruth has red our leters an is going to edit them if that is okay with you. I guess there is copy-right and stuf so let me know if it is okay. She has 2 of yore Leaders books and mummmmmmmmmmmmmmy ses she (Ruth) is the bestest poetry teacher ever. She ust to teach with my mum for abouy 50 yrs and has just moved to a retirement place becuse her husbond is qwite sick. He ritres pomes also and he was a English professer. They both like cats. He had one called

Archie and she had Mama cat, Loopy, Gogol, and millions of kittuns when the first 2 cats had them at the same time. Once she had 16 kittuns and gave them to her students: "This kitten's name is Bplus; this one is A." I gess her students loved cats and was very smart.

URGUNT MESSACGES! You must Not come to see me. It is a verry long way and ruff cuntry. If you walk on the road you would get kilt, lotsa cars going verry fast. And mountains and rivers and ded deer and trafic cops. Then there is Lake Ontario, very coldd with ice snd deeep water and eeels and canada gees (very scary). There are skunks and cayoytes in the city what eat cats and dogs. I was given a scary mask to frighten them but that is a other story.

Our next door dog tries to be nice but he weighs 90 pds and knocks peple over and he is sorry but if our door is open he runs in and gobbles up our food. When anuther family lived next dor, my stoopid brother wuld git up and sleep on the beds and jump up on the dininng room tabul. And licked the butter. The lady was very nice and said, "Thats ok; it is good for his coat" and my mummmmmy sed "he has bad manners and all yor butter is bad for his chlorseterol": and she buyed the lady a coverd buttter dish.

Even if you got here the snow is deepp in the yard and ther is some rough cats around. One we called Mike Tyson ruffed up a lotta cats and a posse of vigilantes took him to the humane society to get done in. Maybe I woud have "found relief"–that is a suthern phrase Laurablle told to mummy who thought it was relief from constipatiun but no—Maybe I will find relief so youd have that long trip for nuthin. Lots of cats yowl around here. 3 seconds after Nik goes out he yowls lowdly. People passing on the street ring the door bel because they think he must be frozen or hurt. And the postman and the snow guy and all thews kids. Daddy says we need a fulltime butler to answer Nik's reqwests.

No, i DONT Wants you to freese and cry like Micel Furrry. Please.

Also I think your name is beautiful and distinguished. The guy in the story was always getting pooped on when he was trying to be nice. He went to the old ladys party and carved the bird. The lady with the broch was very rude to him. He was nice to his wife when she tolt him why she was cring and asked her to wear goloshes. Maybe that sounds nerdy in Carolyna but here they is important. Even the Qween gets sick if she does not wear hers.

StRong, stedy puRRs foR you,

RosemaRy

To: RosemaRy <ProfJaLewis@yahoo.com>
From: Gabriel <JniceFul25@gmail.com>
Date: March 7
Subject: Crafty

My deaR, deaR RosemaRy,

Life has been a little crazy here. Two days ago, my mother discovered we didn't have any hot water. Since then we've had plumbers coming in and out with odd metal contraptions. Neither one of them seems to like cats very much, but at least they've managed to get the hot water heater running again. To be honest, I don't understand why hot water has been such a concern for my mother (and other humans for that matter). Cool water is nice for drinking. If humans could only lick themselves clean, they wouldn't have to have those "showers" they talk about. If they like showers, why don't they just stand outside in the elements like Michael Furey? My two sisters Megan and Alison are arriving for a visit tomorrow. Somehow my mother seems to think hot water is especially important for Megan and the kitten inside. To be clear, the kitten is already floating in her own little pool. She won't care about a water faucet, will she?

An editor for our letters? I feel so important! Don't you? But I wonder if my paws can continue to pounce across these keys to say anything that's worthy of such scrutiny! (I think that's what my mother whines about when she speaks of "writer's block.") Your friend Anty Ruth sounds as if she'll make an exceptional editor. I do want to say, though, that I love your so-called misspellings. I hope we won't lose all of those! They seem so unconventional, almost revolutionary. Remember that William Blake and Emily Dickinson were resolute in defying the tyranny of conventional spelling and punctuation! But I can see that some humans might need help in finding some of your oh-so-charming letters "readable," so maybe a few concessions are in order...

My mother has said that she might one day try to craft a long poem (or even a play) out of our words. (I want to give her an English sniff when she uses the word "craft." As if you and I aren't crafty enough without her intervention... She says she would, of course, get your mother's permission and give her full credit. Honestly, I'm outraged at that comment! What does your mother/leader or mine have to do with any of this? It would be you and I who have to grant consent, you and I who need to be given the credit! I hope I have clarified my position on that issue to everyone!

Thank you for reminding me of my namesake's goodness. I like your "reading" of that character much better than my mother's. I hope I can be as kind and respectful as the Gabriel Conroy you describe. I'm so happy to have my name rehabilitated! Though I have to say, doing something impulsive to show you my devotion does have its appeal. Sadly, you don't have to worry about my making the journey to Toronto. My mother seems to have gotten wind of my plan. A few days ago, I managed to dart out the door. Instead of turning back at the next loft's door, as I usually do, I raced all the way to the back stairs. When I looked back for a second before plunging down the stairs, my mother stamped her feet and shouted at me. It didn't frighten me exactly. I'd say...I was...startled. Yes, I was startled and then disoriented, so disoriented that I ran right back up the hallway and through the doorway into my own loft.

Since then, when she opens the door, my mother blocks all prospect of an exit with her briefcase or her overly large purse. Please, know that it is not cars or dogs or raccoons or coyotes that keep me from coming to you, my dear. No, it's my leader's vigilance. (I usually call her my mother, but her recent tyrannical behavior seems to warrant a harsher term.) When you look out the window, imagine me shivering in the rain and cold. I am there in spirit—a cat with a brain worthy of the name Gabriel but with the valor of a Furey.

My leader/mother says life as we know it is about to change. (She is so prone to hyperbole and drama!) The sisters will soon be here keeping me from the computer for days. Then in a week, my mother will travel to Tennessee to "Match Day" with my sister Alison (apparently a day when she will discover her fate as a doctor). Then the following week she'll jump on a train right across the tracks (without me, of course) and journey to Raleigh where people will shower gifts (not hot water) on the kitten. (Everyone is waiting to see if Megan is "dilated.") During these events, I'll be stuck here in my brick and glass box. Yes, nice cat-sitters will pet me and offer me treats, but I doubt they'll turn on the computer and let me paw away at the keys. Sigh. I hope our correspondence will not be interrupted too much by all these human events. After all, my leader is "she who must be obeyed."

Much love to you my deaR, Resilient sweetheaRt,

Gabe

~

To: Gabriel <JniceFul25@gmail.com>
From: Rosemary <ProfJaLewis@yahoo.com>
Date: March 7
Subject: Feline Duties

DeaR GabRiel:

I am so reliefed. Yes I have found relief (in the positive sense) that circumstances will prevent your traveling here. Your Leader MUST be Obeyed. She is the source of wisdom, kindness, and can openers, the provider of kibble and kittty litter. She loves and protects you. So do I but Im not on the scene and have a limited income. She is faced with plumbers and the end of term and the arrival of the kitten. I want you warm and dry and in your pajamas, not coughing and freezing in my back yard. I appreciates your passion and intentions, but she needs you there to supervise the hot water, look after the house while she is away, and be nice to the family. Id say you must be the man of the family but that's kinda unfemiist. Please note I have cleaned up my spelling and grammmer in case the Leader puts us in a pome or dramuh. I dont wants to look stoopid just becus I am multy-lingual.

You have so much to look after. I qwight understand that keybording is a difficulty. I nowe your hart is studfast and I wil think of you tenderly while yor patriotic dewties engage you for the next shorrt whyle. I too wil be bisy myself; my beautiful fur is growing in and i shd spend some time groooming. Daylite saving switch is starting and that riqwirs many adjustments. So I wil make gooduse of my time, thinking of you and ketching up on my lit6tle tasks here while you guard the homeland while yor Leader is in Raley and Tenahsea. You must think of her and the kittun and matching your doctor-sister to her destiny. Has she kunsidred being a vet? Its an ugly7job but someones got to do it.

So I wont exspekt to have lettrs for a whyle and wil concentrate on metaltellepethy and the powar of are twoo hearts beeting as one til you get yor powerful paws on the computir agin.

Much lov,

yoR faithful sweet-meat,

RosemaRy

To: RosemaRy <ProfJaLewis@yahoo.com>
From: Gabriel <JniceFul25@gmail.com>
Date: March 31
Subject: Maternal Work

DeaRest RosemaRy, my love,

I have missed talking to you so much. My mother has been sick with something called a norovirus and then, for two weeks, bronchitis. Rather than getting well and letting the antibiotics do their work, she has traveled out of town to attend to my sisters Megan and Alison. As I suspected, the cat sitters didn't turn on the computer while she was away. I hope you have not interpreted my silence as a lack of love and concern for you. Before we pick up the flow of words, please tell me that you are well and able to receive my letters.

I wish I could see you with your new beautiful fur. Maybe your human family and friends will bring a picture of you when they drive to Salisbury. I could have my mother fasten it with a magnet to the refrigerator at whisker level so that I could press nose to nose with you every day.

Thank you for sending good wishes for my mother. She has just come back from the doctor's office. She had to have a shot, but she seems less upset by it than I am when the veterinarian doctor gives me a shot. She hopes she'll be able to see your parents and their lovely friends. We both remember all of them fondly. (They let me jump in their laps and climb on their shoulders—exceptionally refined humans.)

Of course, there is a chance she won't be here. Megan's kitten is expected to arrive on April 24, but my mother and Megan's doctor think she may go into the hospital before then. Just now, my mother said this cryptic thing: "Megan is already dilated a centimeter." I have no idea what she means by that. Sometimes I notice the pupils of my eyes are dilated when I look in the mirror after I've been chasing a moth or a fly, but my eyes don't seem to have anything to do with a kitten. Perhaps Megan's eyes are widened with excitement. I'm feeling a little lazy today, but after a long nap I might drag out the OED and see if I can understand this word "dilate" a little more completely.

Don't tell your mother and father this, but I am trying to devise a plan for getting into the car with them and riding to see you. I am mulling over several options. Hiding in one of their bags, purses, or suitcases...Jumping lightly onto their shoulders as they are leaving. (They might not even notice!)

Much love to you, as I imagine your dilated eyes, your silky fur,

GabRiel

~

To: Gabriel <JniceFul25@gmail.com>
From: RosemaRy <ProfJaLewis@yahoo.com>
Date: March 31
Subject: Food and Love

Dear Gabe: I am here on the computer while the rest of the family is in repose waiting for breakfast to appear. Croissant, strawberries, cheese, cold roast beef and coffee for Mummmy. (A spread of food equal to what the aunts prepared for guests in the story called "The Dead.") I am so spoiled that I turns up my nose at anything as plain as cat food. I will get chicken flakes while Nick will get his usual kibble plus some commercial tinned stuff.

I am so sorry yr Leader has been sick. Is she better now? Is anybody else helping you look after her? Or bringing stuff like food and medecin and whisky. She nedes to be ppettud and spiold herself. And I hppe you hav not ben neglected yorsel. Dady has bean bisy opening and heating. stuff. I wish I liked sowerKroat as much as he does. Mummmmy says 2wice a yere is delishus but 3 times a day is a bit much. Mostly I hides it in clevur places but aftur a wwhile it gets somewhat smelly.

Waiting to Read youR woRds,

RosemaRy

To: RosemaRy <ProfJaLewis@yahoo.com>
From: Gabriel <JniceFul25@gmail.com>
Date: March 31
Subject: Feline Medicine

DeaR Rosie,

I am glad you are getting the fine food you deserve, my dear one. My mother just brought in a terrible "original formula" bag of Meow Mix—in other words, the blandest, most pedestrian food imaginable. How does she expect me to dash across the keys, poetic words flowing onto the screen, if she gives me food the masses eat? I suppose I must live vicariously through you, RosemaRy. Linger over your chicken flakes and other delicacies for me, please. I know I sound selfish, but don't worry. I'm trying to help my mother get better. I lie on her feet or stomach at night. When she coughs, I rush to her face and try to suck on her breath to help her. To be honest, I think I'm healing her more than any medications. We must all take care of each other, mustn't we? To think your mother might stay behind if you aren't well. . . Sometimes humans can be almost. . . feline, can't they?

Much love to you, as I imagine your dilated eyes, your silky fur,

GabRiel

~

To: Gabriel <JniceFul25@gmail.com>
From: RosemaRy <ProfJaLewis@yahoo.com>
Date: March 31
Subject: The Perils of Travel

DeaR GabRiel, my love,

My anty Ruth, oure editor has been sik with a operation and pnumonia, but she dusnt want visitors or phone calls or evun messidges frum me so we are anxius aboat her and oar corespondanc must be just siting arouand until she is wel again.

I am wel and my beautiful furr has grown, and I look worthy of yer atencions again. I evan went out on the verandouh when it was sunny out. I don't have a picture of my updated fur. Dadddy bot a camera when Bear was born but hasunt taken pictures since. His hobbies are oftun short-lived. I will ask Laura (Bear's wife) who has lotsa photos. Mummmmmy seys again she wil not cumm to carolyna if I get sik again.

My nefew Joshperson has bean to Yrelund and to all sorts of coleges in the nowrteast to visit to see if he can go to skule their and Mery an Airass with lotsof money. He wood study engineering phisics or logo constuctions or fine-ance so he culd spind the airass's money. His sister has bin playing basketsballs or sockher or something. The dawg Lucy has bean barking and whizzing.

I wood be skard if you hid in a suitcase because youd be stuck in cloths and maybe not recued or letout to whizz or have your supper and you might not have a passport and stuff. And maybe you woodunt get back in time to welcome Maguns Kittun. I think dilated means your open wide eyed. Maybe a muthers eyes dilate so she can see the kittun arriving. I don't remember.

It sounds as if your mummmmmy is not all well so you must purr and take care of her and help with all the end of term marking. Will she go away in the summer? Then you could come and see me if I am still in this life or conventialy reincarnated. If I become a big horse you might be afraid I wood stepp on you with a big hoof. I got to go to bed now so sweet dreeems for both of us (and our people).

Take kare and look aftir yor Leader.

Luvingly with fuRRy hugs, Rosie

To: RosemaRy <ProfJaLewis@yahoo.com>
From: Gabriel <JniceFul25@gmail.com>
Date: April 4
Subject: The Freedom of Travel

Oh, you're right, dear RosemaRy. I don't have a passport! My mother just got hers renewed for her trip this summer to Dublin and Wales—a shorter trip than usual because she doesn't want to be away from Megan's kitten too long. I don't know why she didn't think of getting me a passport too. Of course, my only trip this year (unless I escape) will be in my carrier to the vet's office next week. Maybe I can take one of her old passports and come for a visit this summer. I love that you remind me of our many lives and the possibility of reincarnation. I've never seen a horse before so I don't know if I would be afraid or not. I might be able to ride on your back. We could go on adventures together. . . . It has just occurred to me that I've never seen any animals in the flesh except for all the cats at the shelter.

My mother has been teaching poems by a brooding man named Ted Hughes. She left the book open to a poem about a Jaguar, and I've decide that's what I'd like to return as—a high-powered cat. The poem says that even in a zoo, the jaguar is able to spin "from the bars." It says "there's no cage to him / More than to the visionary his cell: / His stride is wildernesses of freedom." That's what I'll dream of when I nap today—wildernesses of freedom. In my dream I will spin from the bars of this cell I live in, like the jaguar. I will stride free of my cat carrier and race all the way to Canada. I will follow my vision across the border until I reach you, my love. No one will dare ask me for a passport.

Much love,

YouR fieRce GabRiel

~

To: Gabriel <JniceFul25@gmail.com>
From: RosemaRy <ProfJaLewis@yahoo.com>
Date: April 6
Subject: The Perils of Travel, Take Two

Hello again, you lovable Man Cat:

Really you must abandon the idea of coming to Canada on your own but if your Leader can get you a cat passport maybe you could visit during the summer when your Leader is away. Maybe Brien could bring you if he comes here and the dawg stays at home or if my parents come or if an airline ticket doesn't cost very much but you would have to ride in a cat carrier. Your Leader would have to get you to Charlut. My mum could pick you up at the airport in Toronto. There would be my stooped bruther but he dusunt do rough stuff. Today HE PEED on the bed 2wice!!!!!!. The Parental Units had tooked the Shiites off the bed to wash them and he PEED ON THEMATTRUS @2wice. My Daddy sed he wood rinngh his f---- (FURRY????) neck but he diunt and they putt the hairdrier to get wrid of the PEE and sume smelly stuff to smell over the Pee. Nik is lying in a good place til daddy gets bisy with hockey-tennis-basketsballs-baseballs-golf which he watches all-at-1once. My mummy has stopped eating becus its now curling and they are all dopey looking guys with brooms and big rocks and they YELLL. awful. Yesterday they visited Anty Ruth who is feeling better but not all well yet. You must be very busy with all the marking and preparing for Megun's Kitten. I gotta go and see if anything nice is on Mummmys Plate.

xxxxxx

Rosie.

~

To: Gabriel <JniceFul25@gmail.com>
From: RosemaRy <ProfJaLewis@yahoo.com>
Date: April 11
Subject: A Visit

GabRiel my puRRiest: I know you are up to your ears looking after your Leader at term's end, especially with Megan's kittun ready to pop. My parental units are leaving tommoror morning so our typing thing will be turned off.

Maybe my aged parents will catch a glimpse of your Mama or even You!!!! Kisses and Pats via them.

I look qwit well and Rosalyn, my charming governess will take good care of me and my stooopid peeing brother. Laura, my sister-in-law, may find a picture of me for you!!!!!! Pleees delay your plans about a tRip to Toronto until we can arrange a safe route. Your Leader and me would be devastated if you got loooost or injured.

Loving all the fuR on youR pReshust body,

RosemaRy.

~

To: RosemaRy <ProfJaLewis@yahoo.com>
From: Gabriel <JniceFul25@gmail.com>
Date: April 11
Subject: Job Description

Dearest RosemaRy,

My mother has been chasing her tail these days like an obscenely small, yappy dog. She's racing around packing and unpacking her bag for when she gets news that Megan's kitten has started trying to make her appearance. She sleeps with that flat, flickering thing she calls a cell phone in her hand. But what this means is she never relaxes enough to turn on the computer and make way for me. My job I guess these days is to brush my tail against her leg to remind her that I'm nearby if she needs me or if sister Megan needs me. I also sleep on her shoulder and pat her face with my paw while she's dreaming about the kitten.

I'm wondering if your mother and father and their friends have embarked on their journey to North Carolina. Hopefully, they will have a safe journey and you will be well enough for your mother not to mind leaving you. Will someone nice feed you while they're gone? Will someone stop by to clean up any of Nik's "indiscretions"? Is it the "governess"?

Please know that even when I'm not tapping my paws on these keys to send you my love, I am thinking about you as I dart across the beams. I am practicing running along the concourse toward you when I finally arrive in Toronto, my beloved.

WhiskeRs bRistling with love,

GabRiel

VI. EXCURSIONS

To: RosemaRy <ProfJaLewis@yahoo.com>
From: Gabriel <JniceFul25@gmail.com>
Date: April 28
Subject: Pictures of Rosie

Dearest RosemaRy,

My mother is leaving me again to visit the new kitten. The only thing that's keeping me going is that she has placed the beautiful pictures of you where I can see them any time I want. Your face is delicate and sensitive beyond words.

All my love, GabRiel

To: Gabriel <JniceFul25@gmail.com>
From: RosemaRy <ProfJaLewis@yahoo.com>
Date: April 28
Subject: The Approach of Spring

DeaRest GabRiel: I'm glad you like the photographs of moi in my beautiful fur. Actualzy, they were taken a few yeres ago but I stil loooke like that minus the coller. LauRabelle is a real sweet-hart to have fixed them up. I gess she noes how important they aRe to us.

Don't fuss that yor Leader is away playing with Emory; kittuns get a lot of attention because they are little and neede to be loookd aftir. She (the Janicelady) still luves you. You just rest up because being an onkle or an ant rekwires a lot of effort and responsibility. You wil have to teech her to play nicely and to never pull a tail.

My parental units say it was springtime in Sallysberry and now it is almost here. The two-lips is out and then daffydills and the tres is budding-up a little. Lie in the sunbeams, Beach Boy.

With many ruff-tunged kisses, Rosie.

To: RosemaRy <ProfJaLewis@yahoo.com>
From: Gabriel <JniceFul25@gmail.com>
Date: May 5
Subject: Pictures of Gabe

Hello, RosemaRy and eveRyone else (cats and humans alike).

My mother is finally home from her week staying with Emory and Megan and Nate (and their huge boxer Rocky). Apparently, it was a wonderful week, but my mother is completely exhausted. Other people administered her exams while she was gone. She spent the week trying to grade a little during Emory's naps, but honestly she didn't get that much accomplished—academically speaking. But it was a glorious week in human terms. My leader has fallen madly in love with Emory, and I'm proud that Megan is doing so well as a mother. What a great little world they are creating for Emory!

My mother is attaching a few photographs of Emory, including a smiley one while she was in the hospital. She seems to appreciate the hospitality she is receiving.

I'm also including one of me for you, dearest RosemaRy. The cat sitter took it while my mother was away with the kitten and my sister. I'm not beautiful like you, my lovely girl. But I strived to look intelligent and somewhat noble as I posed for the photo, knowing you might see it. Just thinking of you and looking at your mysterious eyes in the photograph make me want to be heroic and creative and magical.

Until the next time I can sneak onto the laptop, I am youR loyal and loving GabRiel.

To: Gabriel <JniceFul25@gmail.com>
From: RosemaRy <ProfJaLewis@yahoo.com>
Date: May 6
Subject: More Pictures

Dearest GabRiel,

My mum said you were gorgeous and you are! heroic! creative! and very magical!!! Just like a unicorn only feline and without a phony-looking horn. You look very noble and intelligent. Your sitter must really like you to catch such a beautiful pose. You look like a champion without the sweat. I adored you for your personality and gracious prose but linked with your physique you are quiet dynamite.

Thank you also for the pictures of Megun and her kiitun. The lattur looks very sweet and smiley for such a teeny one and her eyes are open!!!! She must be very advanced. And Megun looks pretty and smiley too. And she has green eyes like you. Does Allyson look like her? But with a stealthyscope?

You are doing a grate job of helping your Leader finish the marking but maybe you should go with her to Tennysee so she doesn't fall asleep when she is driving. Or she could stay over and somebuddy could dress you up and you could be the College Marchall. You could pull the big stick and walk carefully in the blacl robe. Youd look kinda cute in her mortarbored but not as funny as Bear looks in his hat.

Rest up, my sweet heart. Thanks for yore letter and the pitcures.

Lovingly,

Rosie!

~

To: RosemaRy <ProfJaLewis@yahoo.com>
From: Gabriel <JniceFul25@gmail.com>
Date: May 18
Subject: Delicate Face

DeaRest RosemaRy,

I have so missed our correspondence. You may wonder why I seem to have vanished, and well you should. My mother has been on a series of adventures: carrying the big stick for graduation, returning to visit Megan's kitten for Mother's Day, and, now, preparing to leave for two weeks in Wales on Tuesday.

She has also experienced a few misadventures this week. She had a flat tire in her old humanmobile on Wednesday. Then yesterday she claimed this very computer she uses "crashed." I don't understand what she means. This red computer sat quietly on her desk and showed no signs of moving or making loud sounds. She rushed away with it in the morning to take it to the computer doctor and returned last night with it. Now she says it has new problems--very slow typing, for one thing. I am having no trouble with it using my paws, but I guess human fingers can be faster. It's always something with humans, isn't it?

By contrast, this week I have had contact with the most generous, thoughtful, and beautiful cat the world has known —you! My mother helped me open the package you sent for Emory, and we were dazzled! My sisters Megan and Alison both loved *Anne of Green Gables* when they were kittens. In fact, my mother talked to them about Prince Edward Island and Anne when she took them to Nova Scotia when they were about eight or nine years old (in human years). Now we're all waiting for the new kitten to grow her head large enough to fit into the glorious straw hat and braids.

My mother is debating about whether to keep the book and doll here for Emory's visits, but I have told her she should take them to Raleigh so that the kitten can look at the doll until Megan or my mother can start reading her the book. Unfortunately, my mother won't visit Raleigh for about three weeks, but I think that will be okay. Human kittens are fairly inert and patient. (Right now she seems to stare at the ceiling fan more than anything else.) Thank you, my beloved, for contributing to the kitten's literary advancement. Of course, Anne is much kinder than Gabriel Conroy, but she is just as imaginative and articulate. Kindness, while not as exciting as hauteur and irony, is an acceptable virtue for a kitten.

Before I close, I must return to your beauty. My long-time cat-sitter has just finished her years at the college. She is very sad that we won't spend time together anymore. But, on our last day together, she saw your two photographs. She said, "This is the most beautiful, delicate-faced cat I have ever seen." A less secure cat than I would have been overwhelmed with envy and would have felt slighted. But knowing you are my true love (and agreeing with her assessment of your lovely face), I could not help but compliment her on her discriminating taste.

A new cat-sitter will arrive on Tuesday. My mother has promised to position your pictures where I can see both of them any time I feel lonely. I miss you so much, my dear, and hope you are well.

Much love,

YouR GabRiel

VII. INVASIONS

To: Gabriel <JniceFul25@gmail.com>
From: RosemaRy <ProfJaLewis@yahoo.com>
Date: May 19
Subject: Squirrels, Scrolls, and Pandas

Hello my SweetheaRt:

How wonderful to receive your letter; you and your Leader have had such a busy time. I'm sory to hear about her mechanicul difficulties. With respect, as the lawyers say.

Some news: we have had a domestic invasion and the invader may still be in the basement, pore little bugger. Thurs we heared noisy running in the ceiling, Fri am, a big thump and then scrabling and some urgent little scurries behind a chest of drowers and little urgent squeals and there was a little black squirrel right in the house. My parents put Nik and Me behing a closd door and called Wayne the Rackoon Man who sed squirrels don't bite and tried to get him in a box or grab him in a towel. He said heed callus ritr back. My parents tried but the squirrel was very active and very scared. One of the sunroom doors came open and he runned into the rest of the house. My daady went to wahtch TV and sed we`d never find hin cause we have a big house full of hiding places (I know!!!) And the basement is like the black whole of Calcutta. Wayen the Rman did not callus back.

Mummy went down to the Black Whole basement and there was scurrying on one part behin old trunks with cob-bwebs and old sinks and boxes and flatend out boxes but no sight of the squirrel then or since. So we left the back door opun and put water and sum knuts for him and close the door to upstairs and sumtims Mummmmmy sits at the door with a book and watches to see him. So we don't know. Maybe he ranout without eating the knuts and maybe heès still hiding and scared. If the latter we wish he wood eat the knuts and we wool leave more.

My stooped bruther mostly sits down and looks streat ahead unless there is food or he wants his eares scratched. This morning, newish people across the street phoned to ask Daddy if he had a golden cat. Nik was sitting in the sun in their yard and they were worried so phoned with number of his tag and the humane socity gave them our phone number and daddy went over and got him and actusaly I visited them ages ago and they saw my number and the lady said she remembered rescuing me but she didn't know there were 2 cats and Nik was welcome to stay but 1 of the kids was having a birthday party and it wuld be very noisy. Dadddt thanked her for rounding up Nik and me and said there were no more cats at the moment and Nik sed he wanted to go to the party and daddy brot him home.

When she was little Ana Luise (my niece) heard the blak sea scolls were visiting in Charlote and she wanted to see them. Laura and Bear thot it was odd but they took her to the exhibition and Ana Lo was quiet and when they cumed out she sed, Ididunt see any sqirrels. . . .

There are 2 big Panda Bears at our zoo. They don't speak Englush but if you come to visit we cld go to see them, maybe.

I hope yore Leader has fun in Wales. You will be busy training yore new catsitter. The gone- away one was nice to admire my piktoor. I have yours on the bottom part of our fridge. You probably will have a big job fixing yore computer while yore leader is away.

Im glad Emory will like the doll and her hat even if it is too big at the present.

I dont live near a trainbut I will think of you when I see one on tv. I press my tail to the pictur above the keys and wave it at you on the rafters. Stop being sad becase I think I will outlive the vet. My whiskers brush you with a kiss. Rosie.

I think GabRiel is a lovely name.

Much love,

YoRe RosemaRy.

~

To: Gabriel <JniceFul25@gmail.com>
From: RosemaRy <ProfJaLewis@yahoo.com>
Date: May 19
Subject: More Travel

Other important stuff, Gab-sweetie. Will yore Leader see whales in wales? Or prince Wiliam and Kate? And are you interested in race horses? Very beatyful!! Yesterday Oxbow won a big race and was in front the whole way. Dadddy likes outsiders and his pick called senator or governer something was 2nd to last. Mummy liked Orb the most favorit but he wasunt in the mood and comed in forth. All of them very elegant

Kisses, Rosie

~

To: Gabriel <JniceFul25@gmail.com>
From: RosemaRy <ProfJaLewis@yahoo.com>
Date: May 20
Subject: No Racoon Man

Gabriel, my dear

I gotta be qwick, Mummy says, becus your Leader will need to pack her computer to go and visit the seals and O'Sprays and maybe Whales. We all hopes she relly enjoys her visit.

Be cool and rest up, my Handsome guy and we'll be in touch when she gets back. No sign of the sqwirrel or the Racoon Man.

Love and xss, Rosie

~

To: RosemaRy <ProfJaLewis@yahoo.com>
From: Gabriel <JniceFul25@gmail.com>
Date: May 20
Subject: Seals, Ospreys, and Pandas

Hello, deaRest RosemaRy,

This may end up being my last letter before my mother leaves for Wales. She will take the computer with her because her job in Wales will be to write and to help other writers write. That's why she's especially concerned that the computer is still malfunctioning. She hopes to get more help from the man who worked on the computer on Friday. The computer used to let her see pictures of Megan and the kitten through something called Skype, but now that doesn't work.

I'm glad your parents are kind to the little squirrel that's trapped in the house. I love squirrels. I like to observe them from the window, but, of course, I've never seen one up close. Did the Raccoon Man ever come to help? It pleases me to think that a human would call himself Raccoon Man. Please keep me posted about the squirrel's adventures and misadventures.

We also love horses, but my mother hasn't been able to watch a Triple Crown race since that terrible accident when the lovely horse Barbaro shattered his leg at the Preakness. But we saw Orb on the news after the Derby, and my mother was pulling for him.

My mother has never seen whales in Wales, but she has seen seals, and every year her friends take her to see a pair of rare nesting ospreys who return from Africa to the same tree every year to have their chicks. I wish I could see them too. Life in this loft is fairly limited in terms of experiencing nature and other creatures. Maybe I should have a brother like Nik for company, though, from your description he doesn't seem very companionable. While my mother is away I'll try to devise another escape plan so that I can journey to

Toronto. I will daydream about sitting side by side with you at the panda exhibit.

I will think of you every day, my lovely girl.

Much love,

GabRiel

To: Gabriel <JniceFul25@gmail.com>
From: RosemaRy <ProfJaLewis@yahoo.com>
Date: June 22
Subject: Happy at Home with You

GabRiel, dear one.

Tell your mother welcome home. I hope Wales was terrific and I'm sure Emory has grown in grace and charm and welcomed your mother with many coos and gurgles. And soon your mother is off again. What a busy jet setter! She must be happy to be at home with you for now.

Rosie

To: RosemaRy <ProfJaLewis@yahoo.com>
From: Gabriel <JniceFul25@gmail.com>
Date: June 22
Subject: Daemons and the Dark Materials

Dear RosemaRy,

I have been waiting and waiting for my mother to "get back to her life" so that I could write you. After she returned from Wales and the seals and whales, "not getting back to her life" involved a crashed laptop and setting up a new one and two visits with Megan's new kitten. And now, in a week, she will leave me again to go to the North Carolina mountains to teach at a place called Wildacres.

While she was in Wales, my mother read the first book in a trilogy by Philip Pullman, a writer who grew up in Wales, very near the place where my mother often teaches. The trilogy is entitled *The Dark Materials.* People have been urging my mother to read the books for a long time. The main thing she keeps talking about, now that she has finished the first book, is how each human in the story has an animal companion called a "daemon"—almost like a twin spirit or an alter ego—that never leaves him or her. While the humans are young, their daemons can constantly shift forms from one animal to another in response to what the human might need. The daemon might start the story as an ermine or a snow leopard but then become a firefly when the human is stranded in the dark. Once the humans become adults, their daemons are stuck in one form. My mother keeps talking about how I am her daemon and how I keep her from being alone. She keeps hoping I'll shift into a robin or tortoise and then back into a cat, but I've tried to suggest to her that she is too old to have a shape-shifting daemon. Furthermore, I don't really savor the fact that these "daemons" seem to live in service to their humans. (Clearly, humans live to serve cats. Why doesn't she comprehend this?)

I tell you about this bizarre human piece of fiction to say that I would like you to think of me as your shadow, your twin spirit, your animus that will never leave you. My hope is that thinking this might cause you to feel less alone, my dearest friend and love. I have just brushed my face against your photograph. I hope you felt it.

So veRy much love to you,

Your GabRiel

~

To: Gabriel <JniceFul25@gmail.com>
From: RosemaRy <ProfJaLewis@yahoo.com>
Date: June 22
Subject: Daemons and a Purry Song

Darling boy!

How exciting to hear from you. I'm glad your Leader is home and the kittun is well and you have been thinkings abot me!!! The idea of our tails touching is verrrry exotic (matbe ERotic). And now she is going to Wildacres—wow—are you going?—will you come back a wild cat?

I has had a really tame time since we was in touch (tee hee). As a contrast, I sent you a story of a cat in Alberta where they is all cowboys and oil hunters, no class at all.

I likes the idea of being demonds to each other but not all that bad stuff. My mummmy wil really miss me when I find relief because I sleep on her head and stuff and my daddy likes giving me my medicine becus I don't skrathc and fuss and I sleeps on his chest and purr sometime. He also byes me tasty food.

I got no more news, no more sqwirrels. My muther has a new frind who has a burd named Hugo. We has not met. He has a cage but likes to sit on peoples hands or showlders. Not my mum because she is afraid of birds. I am not afraid of birds excepta mybe eaguls and vultures which i hasnever met. I hope there is not any in the mountains if you go. I am singing you a purry song!

Love, RosemaRy

~

To: RosemaRy <ProfJaLewis@yahoo.com>
From: Gabriel <JniceFul25@gmail.com>
Date: July 2
Subject: Kitten Chaos

DeaRest Rosie,

The last days have been chaotic. My sister Megan visited us. For days, I had to listen to the kitten Emory squawl and mew and laugh, all in what used to be my quiet little world. I must admit, I've never seen a human kitten up close. I was curious. But when I tried to get close enough for a sniff, she'd swing her paws and whack me in the nose. And that awful noise...! I spent a good part of the visit pacing the beams above Emory and the portable crib my mother struggled to assemble for Emory.

Hoping for a quiet love,

Gabe

~

To: GabRiel <JniceFul25@gmail.com>
From: RosemaRy <ProfJaLewis@yahoo.com>
Date: July 2
Subject: Runny-nosed Love

GabRiel deaRest:

Courage, my dear! You have so much to bear! I think that james jyce once sent his love girl, Nora, a bracelet when he was skylarking elsewhere whot said something like "Love is very runny-nosed when love is away" and his bruther (whom was bank-rolling them) said "so is love's bruther." I hope your Muther and her laptop has fun in Wildacres and comes back safely. Every thing is okay here but nuthin is xciting. I didunt know human kittuns is so noisy! Thanks god she wasunt a big litter. Rest up and thanks god for quiet and airscondichuning.

Sweetly,

RosemaRy.

~

To: RosemaRy <ProfJaLewis@yahoo.com>
From: Gabriel <JniceFul25@gmail.com>
Date: July 3
Subject: Alone for Two Weeks

DeaRest Rosie,

Now that that trauma is over, I've discovered my mother is leaving in just a few hours for two weeks in that place in the mountains called Wildacres. (Why are humans set free in a wild place while wild cats like me are trapped in a civilized box? If I could just manage to open one of these giant windows, I'd jump free of my "stoopid" human.)

My "cat-sitter" (who hopefully will not sit on me) will be here late in the day. But she won't have a laptop for me to borrow so that I can write you. I hope she remembers my food! Please don't forget me while I languish here for two weeks. I long to see you, sweet love.

Much love,

GabRiel

~

To: Gabriel <JniceFul25@gmail.com>
From: RosemaRy <ProfJaLewis@yahoo.com>
Date: August 1
Subject: Miles Left on the Speedometer

Dear Gabe,

Thank you for explaining your long silence. I was not ansious and just waited nobley until I got on the keys again. I hope your mother enjoyed her travels and there wasunt bears or big mountin goats to scare her. I hope you will have fun with big kittun Emerry the next time you see her; I guess her eyes are open now. I send my best good wishes to her and her mummy and you. I don't think I have many miles left on my speedometer but I am happy so I don't want you to go all weepy and gnash your teeth.

WRiting love on the screen with the wisp of my tale,

RosemaRy.

To: RosemaRy <ProfJaLewis@yahoo.com>
From: Gabriel <JniceFul25@gmail.com>
Date: August 1
Subject: Yellow Fog

Dear Rosie:

At Wildacres, my mother taught her students some weird poem last week about a man named Prufrock. (Humans use the weirdest names!) She says it's a love song, but it seems like a pretty weak attempt at love. I can do better, can't I? She was trying not to cry when she read me a part of the beginning. Here it is:

> *The yellow fog that rubs its back upon the*
> *window-panes,*
> *The yellow smoke that rubs its muzzle on the*
> *window-panes,*
> *Licked its tongue into the corners of the evening,*

My mother asked me who could love fog and not love a cat. . .and vice versa.

My mother sometimes treats me like I'm one of her silly English majors who likes to sit around and talk and talk about words and poems and metaphors and symbols. But I did like what she said about you and this poem. She says she hopes this will be the way your days end. She hopes you will be gentle like fog or smoke and rub your muzzle against your favorite things and linger over your water bowl and then slip, slip, make a sudden leap and then curl yourself into a soft circle and fall asleep. For a human, she makes sense. Oh, my yellow fog, I am thinking about you with the greatest love,

YouR GabRiel.

~

To: Gabriel <JniceFul25@gmail.com>
From: RosemaRy <ProfJaLewis@yahoo.com>
Date: August 1
Subject: Orange Troubles

DeaR GabRiel of the beautiful fuR,

Yeah, I rememberr that pome about the prufrocked guy who didunt eat peaches. They are okay in a dish but otherwise runny and messy. Another poet wrte about a fog that had litttl cat feet; maybe he ment paws. I have 4 white paws. My stoopid brother has a leg missing so he has 3 paws kinda orange. My muther says he is golden, not Orange.

Do you have the orange lodge in Carolina? They are like the KKK without costumes. My greatgrandmother had Pisbiterian brothers who were very mean and belonged to the oange lodge a long time ago so we arent fond of orange and all the rest were roming catholicks and we diunt like thme either. My father is jewush but was borned in a catlick hospital and the nuns baptizd him just in case. My muthers relatives sum of them wernt enchanted she was marrying a juw but if they had knoed he was also an official cathlick the shit wood hav hit the fan. Brother Brien (Bear) used to be anrican frum the waste up cause he was cristenedd and juish from the waste down cause he was circuscized. One of his frends in high schoool got circuszied and sed he couldunt walk for 3 days; Bear said, too bad when I got circuscied I couldunt walk for a YEAR! That was because when he (Bear) got circuscized he was a little baby and coulundt walk at all for about a year. Babies are not as smart as kittuns. I didn get circuscized because I am a girl but imdid have a histericalectomy so I woodnt have more kittuns. Mummy thot I had had enuff twouble in that direction.

I think GabRiel is a lovely name.

Rosie.

To: RosemaRy <ProfJaLewis@yahoo.com>
From: Gabriel <JniceFul25@gmail.com>
Date: August 1
Subject: Preparing for Another Excursion

Dearest Rosie,

My mother is leaving in a little over an hour to stay for three days with Megan and the kitten. I hesitate to use the word kitten anymore since she now weighs three pounds more than I do. She has made some terrible squawling sounds when she has visited us, but I realize now that I can climb up on the bed or sofa beside her and she won't really do me any harm.

During the last trip, I was staying with an unfamiliar "sitter" (as if I'm a baby or an arm chair!) She doesn't know how to coax me onto the sofa so that she can scratch me in all the loveliest places. Luckily, for this trip, my favorite human companion is driving in from out of town to "take care of me."

How are you feeling, my love? Have you been back to the vet? Are your humans caring for you properly? Are you as lovely (with those liquid eyes) as the version of you that I see right now in my photograph?

My mother has promised to leave me the book your mother sent her about the famous-people cats. Because of the advent of school, she may not get to read it for a while, so she has condescended to let me read it first. She doesn't think I'll appreciate all the cultural icons reincarnated as felines in the book. She has forgotten that I am at least as well read and cultured as she is. I'll leave Jim Morrison to her, but I'll take Chopin. Okay, so my paws can't play the Preludes on our piano, but I have to remind her that her piano teacher used to have to modify some of the chords in the Preludes so that her stubby fingers could play them. That humbles her. I can't wait to read about Abelard and Heloise in the book. (She and I haven't figured out how to do accents on this new computer!) I will think of you, my dear Heloise. I will think of you as I read and wait and sleep.

Much love,

GabRiel

VIII. THE LONG DAY

It hurts me to
know we are both
so lonely without
each other.

To: Gabriel <JniceFul25@gmail.com>
From: RosemaRy <ProfJaLewis@yahoo.com>
Date: August 1
Subject: A Pretty Dress for Rosie

DeaR GabRiel:

How charmin' to receive your letter. I remember you sed your leader and her computer wuld be away so I thoght about you even if you culdnt corespont. I am aware of yore tenderness even without words on the page. I am quite well but lazy so typing big letters is a bit difficult so I mostly uses little ones. Did you ever read about Archie and Mehitable? M was a cat who had a pen friendship with a cockroach named Archie. He (Arch) worked in an office so he could only type at night, and he was so little he couldny type and reach the caps key so all his writing was lower case. At least auto correct will captialize the first letter of each sentenc. I can manage some of the punkstewacion myself unlike Mrs Bloom in the "derty book" as my great uncle Oswald called it.

Not much new around here. I went to the vet to get my clause trimmed—a pet-I-cure, my daddy sed (what a corny guy), and I also went to the cottage. I was so good and stayed inside that my mummy got me a grouchy cat book which has funny pictures and games like draw the dots together. My brother Bear and the others minus the dawg just got back from skylarking around Europe. Last night on tv we saw the Longest movie on tv about the longest day on D day.

Every man in Holywud was in it but too bad jorn wayne and rober Mitchim did not get killed. All kinds of peple got blown up but not in tecknick colour or messily. The gerpersons were the bad guys. Sometimes robert mitchim is the bad guy. Very hard to follow.

I asked Bear to bring me sumthing frum paris and he sed you culd not put mice in a backpack but I didunt want a mice. I sed I wanted a pretty dress, and he sed hed see if there was anything in my size. Nothing yet.

I am now very skinny and mostly sleep in my parunts' bed on top of my mummy's head. Not much traffic there. My daddy found that a "compounding pharmacy" culd make my medicine cheaper than the vet so he got it and there was a perscripion that said Rosemary Louise (cat) on it. So may be it was for anna louise, my bruthers dotter, but I guess not. It sounds as if Emory is quite a hanful (pawful?) now. I hope she treats you with the respet due a uncle. I suphose you don't scratch her if she pulls yer tail.

Don't take that dumb book to seriously. Awful things happened to Abelard, and Hellowease didunt get off to lightly. Maybe you'll have mor fun dressing up as edgarpooh and lamenting me as the Lost Lenoir when I am a gonner. My mummy knowd a girl named Lenore once and she was a real tramp and I don't mean feral.

Love,

Rosie xxxxx

~

To: RosemaRy <ProfJaLewis@yahoo.com>
From: Gabriel <JniceFul25@gmail.com>
Date: August 4
Subject: Correspondence Sustains Me

Dear Rosie, my love,

I hope to hear from you soon. It hurts me to know we are both lonely without each other. Our parents offer us love, but it is not the same as the powerful feline love we share. I think about you all the time. Please write when you get a chance. Our cat-to-cat correspondence sustains me.

With love and patience,

GabRiel

To: Janice Fuller <JniceFul25@gmail.com>
From: Brien Lewis <BearLewis1@gmail.com>
Date: August 4
Subject:

Rosemary passed away peacefully around noon, under the bed, with her head resting on one of mommy's shoes.

To: Janet Lewis<ProfJaLewis@yahoo.com>
From: Janice Fuller <JniceFul25@gmail.com>
Date: August 4
Subject: First Response

Oh, dear Janet and Joe, I am heartbroken to hear this. I was sitting downstairs when I heard my laptop ding its bell, the way it does when a new email arrives, the way in *It's a Wonderful Life* they say a little bell chimes whenever an angel gets its wings. Now that I've read this email, I feel so very heavy sitting in my chair looking at little RosemaRy's picture where it always sits on my desk.

I have not been able to bring myself to tell Gabriel yet. Maybe in a little while I will. I'm glad that he and RosemaRy had a chance to write each other one last time before she left us.

Here is the beginning of a poem that has given me comfort in the past—"The Heaven of Animals" by James Dickey:

Here they are. The soft eyes open.
If they have lived in a wood
It is a wood.

More later...

Janice

~

To: Janice Fuller <JniceFul25@gmail.com>
From: Janet Lewis <ProfJaLewis@yahoo.com>
Date: Aug 4
Subject: Rosemary's Burial

Dear Janice,

Joe dug a spot in the backyard where the forsythia blooms in the spring and we buried her with Gabriel's picture, the Dickey poem and a white rose between her paws and rose petals on top. Joe will pick her a nice stone from the cottage. She's buried a little way from Louise's grave, our first cat when Bear was a little boy.

Joe and I sat down with a small bottle of iced wine, a present from a friend's wedding in 1995, the year Rosie and Nik moved in and toasted a good little cat and a wonderful companion. We watched a bit of The Tempest with Helen Mirren on TV—a fortunate choice: romance, magic and return.

Much love to all of you,

Janet.

~

To: Gabriel <Jnice25Ful@Gmail.com>
From: Janet Lewis <ProfJaLewis@yahoo.com>
Date: August 4
Subject: Don't Stay Sad

Dear Gabriel: Perhaps your mother has told you the news or let you read my letter. I just wanted to let you know how much your love and letters and enthusiasm and romantic ideas meant to Rosie. Because of you she was convinced she was young and frisky, not an old cougar. She loved getting your new and gentlemanly mushy stuff and showing off your picture. She was mostly a happy cat but your love gave her a Rosy Glow. Only you could have done that and her happiness cheered everyone around her.

I know you will feel sad, but please don't stay sad. Think about your mother hearing angel wings and Rosie picking her own beautiful sunny day to take off— and an important day too—the Queen mother's birthday (and she lived to be 104!) and the 99th anniversary of WW1, the abrupt end of the golden Edwardian summer another landmark and, if we believe in cat lore, the launching of another cat life and seven more after it. So run across the piano keys, toss another catnip mouse in the air and celebrate the memory of Superb Cat.

Much love from Joe and me; we'll see you when we get allowed back to Salisbury.

Janet

~

To: Janet Lewis <ProfJaLewis@yahoo.com>
From: Janice Fuller <JniceFul25@gmail.com>
Date: August 4
Subject: Tears

Dear Janet,

Your description of RosemaRy's burial made me cry for the third time today—the first time when I called Megan to tell her the news and the second time when I called Gabriel's favorite cat-sitter to tell her. I finally told Gabriel the news about his sweet love. Neither one of us felt up to doing anything after that. We took a long nap together. Gabe normally sleeps on my feet, but this afternoon he slept on the pillow beside my head. He's still sleeping now. I think he will probably write to you later. I think he's trying to dream about RosemaRy right now.

Here's a hug,

Janice

To: Janice Fuller <JniceFul25@gmail.com>
From: Janet Lewis <ProfJaLewis@yahoo.com>
Date: August 4
Subject: Wild Violets

Janice, what a sweet-hearted creature you are! No wonder you have such amazin' offspring, friends, and, especially, a companion cat.

Joe was the hero who got the shovel moving in the backyard. He didn't want to deliver her to the Humane Society. Our backyard is a northern jungle of weeds, mostly believe it or not overgrown with wild violets stolen from the cemetery where Mozart is buried and illegally smuggled into Canada by a musical next door neighbour. Our late dog, Samantha Bowser-Lewis, watered them faithfully.

Dry your tears, dear little Marshall. Remember how happy Rosie made us, and don't let Gabriel mourn. Rosie isn't under a graveyard in the west of Ireland; she is snug and comfortable in a shady spot, perhaps making friends with Louise. Years ago, when Louise moved in, the boy Brien named her.

Janet

~

To: Janet Lewis <ProfJaLewis@yahoo.com>; Joe Lewis <ProfJoLewis@yahoo.com>
From: Janice <JniceFul25@gmail.com>
Date: August 4
Subject: Last Letter

Dear human parents of RosemaRy,

I am sending my last letter to RosemaRy to you. But I want you to know that I am sending it directly to her by another means. Many months ago, Rosie suggested that there might be something like Celestial Google by which I might send her a message. Sure enough, my well-meaning and sometimes resourceful mother searched the computer until she found Celestial Google. Once she did, I pawed these words into the search box: "RosemaRy, a frisky, always young, hilariously funny, romantic, and sexy Canadian cat." Only one result came up—a strange portal with light streaming from it. Once I finish the letter below, my mother has promised to copy and paste it into that portal. I believe with all my heart that these words will reach my beloved and she will know what is in my heart, now overflowing with love and sadness.

Thank you for all the love you gave to your dear girl. No humans could have given her a better life.

Love,

GabRiel

~

Attachment:

My dearest RosemaRy,

I know that you will already know every word I am about to say to you, but I need to put my paws to keys anyway. I think it will give me some peace.

I am sending a photograph that my favorite cat-sitter took of me while my mother was gone to the beach. As you can see, I am sitting at the window looking out. As I looked out, I was imagining what I have imagined again and again these past months—crossing the railroad tracks and boarding a train for the country where you used to live. I know you were afraid that something bad would happen to me if I attempted the long journey to find you, and I promised I wouldn't try it. But that doesn't mean that I didn't dream of what it would be like to make the trip to finally be able to curl against you.

As soon as she returned, my mother let me read your last email to me. I laughed and laughed at parts of what you wrote—like when you said it was too bad John Wayne didn't die in the movie and when you told me your father talked about a pet-I-cure. I will smile every time my mother tries to hold me down to trim my claws. I will miss your sense of humor and your cleverness so very much. How could one cat have been so lovely and so wickedly smart at the same time?

I know that if I were to get on the train now, I wouldn't find you, not in the form that I came to love in your pictures. My mother read me a poem today about animal heaven. Poets know so little about anything, but I would like to think that this man James Dickey before he died himself came to imagine the place where you are right now. That is how I will think of you as long as I am alive myself—lightning quick with claws as sharp as knives, pouncing and catching more mice than I can imagine. You may not have gotten a London mouse coming in a backpack through customs, but in our heaven you will find one at every turn. You will never be hungry. But you will never need to eat. In fact, after you catch the quickest mouse, you will be able to smile at him and set him free. And there will be a kind pillow just like the one your mother lays her head on every night when she dreams of you and a pair of her softest shoes for you to rest your head on. You will meet the lovely cats who came before us—Louise and my mother's crazy cat McKenzie (who is now sane and doesn't need Prozac).

I have been looking out the window in the hours since I took a nap with my mother. Remember how, those many months ago, I talked about the way I would look for you in Walt Whitman's grass and James Joyce's snow after you were gone? That was so many months ago, and I will always be grateful that what the vet thought would be days turned into months. How lucky I have been to have your love and humor and grace in my life. Today, as I looked out the window, there was no snow, no rain like the cold rain that fell on Michael Furey—only sunshine and a flock of birds flying in formation. Not Canada geese, I wouldn't think, but some kind of birds. I wonder if one of them is you on your way to our poetry heaven. My mother wrote a poem about visiting her mother's grave late in the day she was buried. A big crow jumped from one headstone to another and looked at her and cawed and looked at her again. My mother will always believe her mother had stopped by for one last look at her before she journeyed to some other place. In these next hours, I will look for you passing by my window to get one real look at me before you go. I have cleaned my fur so that I will be handsome when you glimpse me.

Please don't forget me. I will never forget you. One day, if I'm lucky, I'll join you in that place. You didn't get the dress you wished for at the end, did you? I will make you a dress of spider webs and moth wings—the prettiest dress anyone has ever seen. And I'll bring it when I come to meet you. As sad as I will be to leave my mother, I will be so glad for us to take up where we left off, to finish what we were never able to begin—tumbling and chasing and catching, brushing whiskers and tails, curling our arced selves together when we sleep, our two halves now a perfect ring.

With love,

GabRiel

ACKNOWLEDGMENTS

While this book is a tribute to what two cats taught Janet Lewis and me, I also owe a debt of gratitude to quite a few humans.

First, I must thank illustrator and book designer Lauren Faulkenberry. These illustrations have enlivened the emails and helped me discover many trends and themes as I mined the emails Janet and I had written. With her help, Gabe and Rosie came to life on the page in ways they wouldn't have otherwise. Our collaboration was a serendipity that taught me lessons I didn't know I needed.

Much love and many thanks to my family—my twins (Megan and Alison), my grandchildren (Emory and Ellis), and my son-in-law (Nate)—for their enthusiasm and love.

Many thanks to Julia Grimes Hayes and Bill Spencer for carefully reading and proofreading the manuscript and to my friend Angela Overcash for her encouragement during my work on this project. My gratitude to David Pulleyblank, Beverly Connor, and Sean Meyers for securing most of the photos used in this book. Thank you to Lewis Krider for sharing his regular doses of the joy and hope needed to carry on. Thanks to everyone at Wildacres Retreat for offering an inspiring place for working on the book and to my Wildacres friends Judith Hill, Carolyn Elkins, Debra Daniel, Lee Zacharias, and Mamie Potter for providing encouragement and suggestions. A special thank you to Pat Hefner for her unwavering love of Gabriel.

I send heartfelt gratitude to the Lewis family—Joe, Brien, Laura, Josh, Anna Louise, dog Lucy, Molly Cat, and all the animals they rescued and cared for over the years. The human members of the family were great readers of the emails back when the two cats—Gabriel and Rosemary—exchanged them. I couldn't have been the cats' editor if the Lewises hadn't allowed me the literary freedom to mold the emails into this creation.

Janet Lewis wrote half of this book (or at least her cat Rosemary did). Janet and I had often discussed trying to publish the emails. We were giddy as Rosemary and Gabriel continued to surprise us with the way they couched longings, joy, and fear in cat talk and literary allusions. They spoke of big ideas and little pleasures—lying on a pillow next to a human, merging with sunbeams, eating morsels of table food. In a time when Janet and I struggled with our own human maladies, the cats' dreams of transcending geographic and biological limits gave us hope. Ironically, or perhaps appropriately, what gave me the impetus to start working on this manuscript was Janet's wake in Toronto: One of her best friends--Ruth Grogan--read the ending of the email exchange as part of her tribute to Janet. She explained that everyone who loved Janet valued her audacious wit. She lamented that no one had recorded Janet's spoken monologues but hoped that reading the emails allowed Janet's friends and family to remember their Janet and her irreverent sense of humor.

We had fun embarking on this journey from North Carolina to Toronto to Dublin and County Clare. I hope our readers have hidden in a suitcase and traveled with us.

ABOUT THE AUTHORS

Janet Elizabeth O'Brien grew up in Ottawa, Ontario, Canada's Capital. She graduated in Honours English, from Carleton University, as winner of "The Senate Medal" She went on to do graduate work in English at the University of Toronto, where she wrote her Master's Thesis on Chaucer's "Wife of Bath" and her PhD thesis on "The Wasteland Theme" in Joyce's *Ulysses*. While at U of T, Janet studied under the great Northrop Frye, as well as Marshall McLuhan, who served as second reader on her PhD thesis.

In June 1966 Janet married Joe Lewis, a young lawyer practicing in Toronto. Their only child Brien was born in 1967. Janet began her almost forty-year teaching career at York University, Over the years she served as a member of the York Senate, Director of Undergraduate Studies in the English department, and Associate Dean of Education but was most happy in her role as teacher. Her love of teaching can be attested to by so many of her former students, who continued to stay in touch with Janet, long after their graduation.

~

Janice Moore Fuller grew up in North Carolina and raised her twins Megan and Alison in Salisbury. She received her bachelor's degree in music and English from Duke University, where she was an Angier B. Duke Scholar. She earned her MA and PhD in English from the University of North Carolina Greensboro.

She has published four poetry collections, including *Séance* from Iris Press, winner of the 2008 Oscar Arnold Young Award for the outstanding North Carolina poetry book. Her plays and libretti, including a stage adaptation of Faulkner's novel *As I Lay Dying,* have been produced at Catawba College's Hedrick Theatre, BareBones Theater's New Play Festival, the Minneapolis Fringe Festival, Estonia's Polli Talu Centre, and France's Rendez-Vous Musique Nouvelle.

Janice is Professor Emerita at Catawba, where she served as Writer-in-Residence, Professor of English, and Weaver Endowed Chair of Humanities. She was awarded the Trustee Award and the Faculty Senate's Swink Prize for teaching and was selected Professor of the Year five times by popular vote of the students.

~

Originally from South Carolina, Lauren Faulkenberry is a novelist, artist, and cat lover. She earned her MFA in Creative Writing from Georgia College & State University and her MFA in Book Arts from The University of Alabama, where she was a Windgate Fellow.

She is author of the Bayou Sabine series and the forthcoming novel *Rare Birds of Carolina*. Her artist books, which are lovingly letterpress printed, are held in a number of special collections libraries.

When she isn't writing, she is often printing woodcuts on her old Vandercook #1 proofing press. Her fiction is always informed by her eclectic job history, which includes working as a field archaeologist, a printmaking instructor, and a ranger for the National Park Service.

She currently lives in North Carolina, where she is working on a new series and an essay collection.

Top: Rosemary outside in the garden. *Bottom*: Rosemary sits at the window, one of her favorite spots.

Top: Rosemary's family. *Bottom:* Janet and rescue dog Samantha Bowser-Lewis.

Top: Janet. *Bottom:* Janice and Gabriel.

Top: Gabriel. *Bottom:* Janice with her family.

Rosemary in her later years.

CPSIA information can be obtained
at www.ICGtesting.com
Printed in the USA
BVHW031309051020
590321BV00001B/105